Bernard A. Pendry is 85 years young. This is his first novel, aided by his 3rd wife, Sue, 25 years junior to him and eldest son, Mark. Life is good.

Where he got the idea for this novel is a mystery, certainly nothing in his life resembled anything like the goings on in this novel.

He qualified as a Chartered accountant in 1959, second most boring job to an actuary, the highlight was acting for Joe Cocker and going on a tour of the United States with him in 1972. He managed to retire at age 54. In the ensuing 29 years he has done little except amicably divorce his first wife, Sheila, married his second wife, Pam, who he lost to the dreaded C in 2013, got back together with is third wife, Sue, after a parting of 33 years and had lots of fun with his three children and grandchildren.

After giving up, or rather they gave him up, squash, skiing, tennis, he lingers on with golf and snooker at The Royal Automobile Club, plus croquet and electric cycling with Sue.

He has this knack of knowing he is always right, like Clough he may listen to others point of view then tell them they are wrong. He is famed in the family for changing rules if he thinks he can improve them, or if he is not winning!

Apart from publishing a book about his friendship with Joe Cocker, this his first attempt at a novel.

Both my wife, Sue and son, Mark for checking my
terminology and sequence of events.

Bernard A. Pendry

Amanda – A Would-Be Killer

AUSTIN MACAULEY PUBLISHERS™

LONDON • CAMBRIDGE • NEW YORK • SHARJAH

A CIP catalogue record for this title is available from the British Library.

ISBN 9781398404724 (Paperback)
ISBN 9781528969239 (ePub e-book)

www.austinmacauley.com

First Published 2022
Austin Macauley Publishers Ltd®
1 Canada Square
Canary Wharf
London
E14 5AA

Table of Contents

Characters

Amanda Colt, main character and vivacious wife of Harry.

Harry Colt, devoted husband of Amanda.

Simon McFarlane, an old university chum. One hell of a good-looking guy and well connected who went into partnership with Harry.

Bert Hemmings, Night managAer of The Hotel part of The Maddox Hotel Group.

"Your Troubles Solved 24/7" – the name of Harry & Simon's business.

Joe Payne, Auditor of the business.

Mr Len Harvey, MD of The Maddox Hotel Group.

Max, one of the "lovers" visiting the Hotel.

Anita & Kim, ladies who visit The Hotel to give their services.

Herbert C. Malone (Herbie), Private investigator.

George, right hand man of Herbie.

Alias, Bill Smith, information gatherer for Herbie.

Ben Harris, owner of Best One Ltd and Amanda's boss.

W K Althorp known as Mr J.

Zoe, a Latvian woman.

Natasha, sister of Zoe.

The Wimborne Club and Rosebury Manor. Owned by Simon and others.

Jim Carter, head of The Serious Crime Squad. The first five chapters set the scene. The action doesn't take place until chapter six.

Chapter 1

Amanda

Amanda, What a girl! Petite with a smile like an angel who loved entertaining anyone who would listen. Her early life was fashioned by her parents. Mum taught her all those things a young lady should know, how to behave, how to dress, be polite and much influenced by their regular visits to the cinema. The Great Gatsby, being the film, that impressed her most about style. She wouldn't admit that Dad was her favourite, although she sat in wonder at the stories he told about his exploits in the war, which she took as true but in later life took them with a pinch of salt.

They lived in a quaint cottage in the village of Diddington in the wilds of Somerset, where she attended Elmcroft Girls School, a quite forbidding building resembling an abandoned monastery. She adapted to school life like a duck to water, enjoying the camaraderie of fellow pupils and learning so many topics. Her favourite being geography and the world around her. It was here that she got into sports, but not until the 5th grade did she achieve any honours, winning the Elmcroft Tennis tournament.

Lucy was her best friend, they had so much in common always discussing fashion, comparing bust sizes, what they wanted to do when they left school and what it would be like to have a boyfriend.

One day, when her parents had gone to a county show, Lucy came round to the cottage to listen to music. They cuddled up on the sofa and, with no intention, kissed having not done so before. This had an unsuspecting effect, they wanted to try on some other clothes in her bedroom where they stripped off naked then trying on, what they thought was sexy underwear. One thing led to another, more kissing with hands exploring each other's bodies. Shocked they sat giggling saying, "Are we lesbians?"

"No just happy friends."

It wasn't long before Amanda started dating a local lad, George, mainly meeting in the village coffee shop, where they discussed things like how the local football team were fairing, popular music, their favourite group being 'The Bay City Rollers', and the recent dance crazes. It was after they attended a disco in the village hall, it happened. Although, still under age, they had consumed a fair amount of alcohol that they blamed for what happened. It was a balmy summers evening and they were walking home across the local park. They stopped to kiss and his hands were all over her to which she reciprocated. They lay on the ground and the conversation went something like this:

Amanda. "George have you ever had sex?"

George. "No but I've always thought of it."

Amanda. "I wonder what it's like?"

George. "Everyone says it's fun. Do you think we should try it?"

Amanda. "I'm willing if you are."

Gently they had intercourse. Post intercourse the conversation went something like,

George. "Amanda I hope I didn't hurt you."

Amanda. "Not really but it was over so quick I don't think we should do it again."

George. "I agree it wasn't like I thought it would be."

And home they went.

It wasn't long after this that her happy life was shattered. It was on the way home from ballet practice in the village hall that two guys grabbed her and bundled her into a small van. She screamed and fought like a tigress, but they were too strong. One held her while the other drove the van out of the village to nearby woods. They threw her to the ground and to stop her screaming and yelling threatened her with a knife. She never stopped struggling when they tried to remove her clothes; one of them had taken his trousers off obviously intending to rape her. Remembering what she had seen in a film, she stuck her fingers deep into the eyes of the guy holding the knife causing him to scream, "You cow! I'm blinded." With that she jumped up and ran for her life, the trouser-less guy not wanting to chase. She hid in bushes until the guys drove off, then she found her clothes and took a long walk back home.

She went straight to her bedroom, her parents having retired, to consider what she should do. Her thoughts went thus, *They didn't rape me but not for the want of trying, if I go to the police I'll get involved in possibly a lengthy court case that will be in the local papers so no, should I tell my parents, this would only upset them so no, I know I will get revenge. I think I recognised them from the local sports club.*

She carried out this threat, traced both the guys, borrowed a baseball bat from George and in two separate incidences battered both of them. She felt retribution had been done, the only worry was there could be some repercussion. Fortunately, there were none.

She graduated from St. Hilda's with distinction. After discussing her future with her proud parents, it was decided the best course was university after which she chose a career.

University

University life took some time getting used to, coming from an all-girls school, there were now as many boys as girls, but segregated in the halls of residence. She adapted quickly to life in university and was thrilled with the sports facilities. It was while entering a doubles tennis tournament that she was paired with this guy Harry, and their first round opponents were a girl named Lucy and her partner Simon.

It was a very competitive match won on a tiebreak in the third. She thought the two men were attractive and gladly accepted their invite for dinner. The conversation was sparking, so many anecdotes, true or imaginary from their lives resulted in howls of laughter.

These guys were great fun and immediately there was a bonding. Soon they became known as The Great Triumvirate, leaders in fashion, outrageous party goers, dominant in sports and envied for their exciting life style.

It was while the three of them were holidaying on the Isle of Granada that the love/sex interest reared its head. Sun, sea, lavish dining, exotic drinks, music, dancing, hot steamy nights, was it any wonder that they threw inhibitions to the wind and she spent nights sleeping with either of them which in effect bonded their relationship even more.

It was while at university that she became a prominent member of both the chess club and gun club. She had no idea how powerful it felt handling a revolver. She got so proficient that she represented the university in various competitions.

Her main academic achievement was earning her PHD in Leisure and Tourism, and this was the direction she hoped her future was heading.

All good things must come to an end so it was 'Goodbye University' and out into the big wide world.

Employments

Through one of Mum's friends, she got a job as a copywriter at the women's fashion magazine, Chit Chat. It wasn't long before she started climbing the ladder, becoming the deputy fashion editor commanding a decent salary. At a promotional trade exhibition, she met Ben Harvey, the managing director of an advertising/marketing company, he was so impressed with her presentation, her winning smile, her soft but positive voice that he offered her a job as advertising manager in his company at a vastly increased salary, with promises of greater involvement. She took to Ben, his casual manner, encouraging dialogue to say nothing of his good looks.

This new challenge with the increased salary was irresistible, so with a sad heart she gave in her notice to Chit Chat thanking them for the experience gained during the time with them.

She had no idea of the traumatic times that lay ahead.

Chapter 2

Harry

Harry was the type of boy you either loved or hated, with his cherubic smile, he looked an angel but when you saw the delight he got from upsetting others like tripping them over or pushing them into nettles, you realized there was another side to his character. Another thing that did not go down well with his classmates was how he excelled at everything, academics, sports, and the arts and how he went on and on about how clever he was. One of his classmates took exception when Harry put a slug in his food box and took a punch at him, hitting him on the side of his face. Harry ducked but in the scuffle, that followed he got a bloody nose and a dented pride.

Much of this could be put down to his parents, as being an only child they lavished money on his education and any sports equipment he desired. Dad saw him as being a leading athlete or sportsman and, being a no mean tennis player himself, enrolled him in the local athletic club. It was here he developed a muscular body and honed his skills.

At age 14, he won a sports scholarship to a higher education college, where he learnt a hard lesson, nobody was interested in his academic achievement, it took some time before he accepted just being one of the boys, a definite character improvement. However, the school welcomed his sporting qualities, mainly for tennis and middle distance running in which he represented the school in local and national competitions.

It was on a school trip to the Science Museum in London that he became overawed by the wonders that abounded, the inventors like Isambard, Kingston, Brunel and Robert Stevenson. He spent hours reading up about these clever people and a particular subject they all excelled in was mathematics. This was to set the direction for his future.

University

The first thing he found strange was there were beautiful girls all over the place. Never before had he had any meaningful contact with the opposite sex so he felt very awkward conversing with them. However, he soon realised they could be as much or more fun than boys.

Apart from throwing himself into his studies, he wanted to further his prowess in sports, especially tennis. It was at the Sports Centre that he met Amanda when he was paired with her against Lucy and partner Simon, who was resident in the same housing. Subsequently they spent many happy hours in each other's company including a holiday in the Isle of Granada, where a love tussle seemed to develop as to who Amada liked best, him or Simon. Nothing was decided but he knew Amanda was the girl for him. Apart from this, they all got on famously and a long friendship developed.

The desire to study all forms of engineering resulted him in getting degrees in Civil, Mechanical, Electrical and Environmental degrees with honours.

Now Out into the Big Wide World

His C.V. was impressive which the university sent to many leading companies in the appropriate field to which he received a few offers. The one that impressed him was from Bromley & Hitchcock Limited, because they specialised in the service industry with clients throughout Europe and the Middle East. They were caring employers, with a good training regime including many residential courses. After 7 years, he was their senior technician in charge of a team of over 50, with responsibility for 100 clients worldwide.

During these years his courtship with Amanda flourished with many ideas in common, they enjoyed reading the same books, went to ballroom dancing lessons, found they had the same taste in films, were always laughing at silly jokes, were very tactile and sex was great. After 3 years together, in a taxi ride to see 'The Mousetrap' in a London theatre, he got down on one knee and proposed, she gleefully accepted the diamond ring that he had bought from Tiffanies, and was placed on her finger.

Soon they rented an apartment in Balham, south London which they enjoyed furnishing, discussing colours, furniture and all things necessary. A couple of years later they married. What a wonderful affair all paid for by her father, Richard, who no doubt thought back to his own wedding that had been paid for by his father. He felt proud walking his daughter, who looked resplendent in a classic off the shoulder gown that highlighted her beauty to the fullest extent, down the aisle. Staring into each other's eyes, they both said, "I do." with such passion; the vicar now said,

"You may now kiss the bride." to a great cheer from the congregation. The reception for the congregation of 120 was at Sheridan's Restaurant where they were served an incredible 5-course dinner washed down with a quantity of champagne. A highlight of the occasion was the hilarious speech of the best man, Simon, who had flown over from Norway. The story that got the loudest laugh was about Harry. After an evening of drinking and dancing at a university ball, he somehow lost his trousers or rather they had been spirited away, such that he had no option other than to run the gauntlet across the dance floor heading for his car.

At midnight a limousine collected the happy couple and drove them to The Ramada Hotel at Gatwick where they stayed the night ready for the next day flight to Granada.

To rekindle old memories, they honeymooned in Granada but this time at the five-star 'Blue Horizon Resort'. What fun it was, not that it was necessary but the marriage was consummated and they made use of all the hotels facilities playing lots of tennis but their main enjoyment was scuba diving amongst the coral reefs, where they were overwhelmed by the myriad of brightly coloured fish, if only they knew their names.

Life looked good, both careers in comfort zone, financially secure so what could go wrong?

An e-mail invite for Harry and Amanda to join Simon for lunch at Simpsons in the Strand.

Chapter 3

Simon

Simon's parents were in the military. His father, a major in the army, so until university, he never lived in the same place for long, and most of the time he was farmed out to a variety of boarding schools. Although he was a bit of a loner, it didn't take him long to learn what fellow pupils desired, starting with sweets and toys, and graduating to cigarettes and a gamble. Using his regular allowance he set about satisfying these needs to profitable effect. He was expelled from one school when he was discovered taking bets on the Grand National. A tongue lashing from his father had little effect and his profitable activities continued.

His education had been a bit chaotic with numerous schools aided by private teachers, which enabled him to achieve sufficient good exam results. He had no interest in further education but with a little coercing from his father, he agreed to apply for entry to a university. He was wary of university, believing he would not fit in thinking that those knew him long to realise the truth, they were all just ordinary people trying to get on. So why not start some of his old habits and get a few pupils fancying their chances on the gee gees.

It was quite amazing how the results invariably came out in his favour.

He found all aspects of university life interesting especially after joining up with Amanda and Harry. They had such fun and perpetrated many pranks on teachers and fellow pupils alike. He was on the same degree course as Harry, soon realising he was second best. However, they both passed with flying colours.

Leaving university he had to think about a career, the careers officer had suggested he enquire about joining the Civil Service. How terribly boring. Reading 'The Times', an advert for a trainee manager of a leisure resort in Norway attracted his attention. He was fortunate to get an offer to attend an all-expenses paid interview in Oslo. The interview with Carl Larson, who introduced himself as managing director (Simon's first thoughts were that he seemed so young for such a position but his appearance and cultured voice were impressive) seemed to go well and whether there were no other interviewees, he duly got the job. They provided a small apartment in the outskirts of Oslo, so commuting was no hardship. He started this first employment just a week later and with minimal training he found the work easy, allowing him lots of spare time much of which was spent in his local bar, Renoirs, getting to know the locals.

The day before he left the shores of England, he had invited Amanda and Harry to join him for dinner at Simpsons in the Strand. Unfortunately, Harry was away on business, so it was just he and Amanda. He changed the venue to Jules Night Club a swanky, intimate place frequented by the jet set. He dressed for the occasion in his Armani casual suit hoping to impress. When Amanda arrived he was flabbergasted, she looked fabulous.

The evening seemed to fly by with superb food, lots of reminiscing, dancing, he loved holding her in his arms, champagne and soon it was 1:30am. He suggested that she should come back to his place for a nightcap, she was tempted realising what would follow, a repeat of the sessions they had on that Caribbean holiday. It took her sometime to decide but said it was late and she had to be early for work so reluctantly Simon called her a taxi.

Although the pay was reasonable, Simon thought, there must be ways to supplement his salary. In his local bar he got chatting to a stranger, Chad Dawson, an old boy who looked like a withered old sea dog, and the conversation turned about the high price of cigarettes compared to the comparatively cheap price in Spain. Chad said he had given much thought to how to exploit the situation and let Simon know he had a villa in Marbella that could be used. He put a deal to Simon; if Simon could set up a team to illegally import cigarettes he would supply whatever finance was necessary and they could split the profits 50/50.

With great caution Simon made enquires down at the docks and after speaking to many people found a couple of long distance lorry drivers who work for a local company and regularly transported goods between the two countries. It was surprising how keen they were to do a deal and said there would be no customs problem as they had been doing a similar venture for some time. Chad put up the money and trade flourished with profits rolling in which were split 50/50. It didn't take Simon long to question why Chad should get half and with no consultation his initial investment was returned and his involvement terminated. Arguments followed but what could Chad do, go to the police? Out of the question.

Simon's eyes lit up when a beautiful lady entered the bar. It didn't take him long to introduce himself and offer to buy her a drink. "Hi, I'm Rosanne but friends call me Roz. Yes, I would love a drink, the house red wine, please." It was not long before they started sleeping together. She was a bit elusive when he asked her what work she did, but after a few drinks and some in-depth discussion she admitted she was a prostitute. This didn't put Simon off in the least and when she said she lived with two other ladies in rather a squalid flat his mind went into over drive. He met with the three of them and put deal for them to consider. He would rent a three bedroomed apartment on the outskirts of Oslo that they could use for their trade, which he would advertise, provided they gave him 25% of everything they earned. They were sceptical but agreed to go for it once Simon had rented a flat. This he did and trade went well up to the time he returned to England. By that time the 'ladies' had sufficient funds to take over the renting of the apartment.

When he got the invite to be Harry's Best Man, he was thrilled and started making plans for how he would carry out his duties, arranging the stag do, gifts for the bridesmaids, his speech and travel arrangements. It all worked like clockwork but when he was standing there during the ceremony he had pangs of regret, had he not gone abroad could it have been him next to Amanda? One will never know.

With eyes on the future he realised that the only way to make big money was in property not only for rental income but the ever-increasing market values. After extensive research he decided that the best buys were small houses on the outskirts of Manchester, so he took a vacation there. He visited many estate agents, discussing the possibilities, until he found one that was prepared to do a deal to put 'certain' properties his way. Next he located a mortgage broker who was not too hot on the rules and would get him mortgages within reason. Even with his limited funds it didn't take him long to acquire six 2/3 bedroomed houses, the rents of which more than covered the mortgage repayments.

During a cruise around the Mediterranean, Simon had formed a friendship with Len Harvey, who shared the same dining table. It was obvious that Len had money. They were staying at an executive suit, his wife Diane displaying a few diamonds, always a bottle of Dom Perignon for dinner and he had the appearance of a contented man, wavy jet-black hair, piercing grey eyes that held your attention, and a broad smile that made you feel at ease. During their many conversations, Simon found out that Len was the managing director of The Maddox Hotel Group that owned six 5-star hotels in and around London. The business was good, apart from the constant problems they were experiencing with maintenance of the services, lifts, air conditioning, heating etc. Of course Simon's ears prick up, could there be an opening here? He mentioned to Len his expertise in this field and they agreed to meet up when they got home.

It was now time to go home, cleared up everything in Norway said goodbye to the locals and off.

Chapter 4
The New Business

Amanda and Harry were surprised to receive an e-mail from Simon, inviting them to lunch at 'Simpson in the Strand' with no explanation of why, so they assumed it would just be catching up on what had happened since last time they met.

Of course they look forward to meeting up and the lunch was fantastic as it always is at this establishment, finishing with their joint favourite dessert, bread & butter pudding with lashings of custard, all washed down with champagne.

Conversations had been very convivial, even joyous mulling over old times with Simon telling them of his exploits in Norway and how he had invested in the Manchester properties. Then he got down to the real point of why he wanted to meet up. He mentioned how he had met Len Harvey the MD of The Maddox Hotel Group while on a cruise, learning of the problems they encountered with relation to their mechanical services in all their six hotels. He had mentioned to Len Harvey their expertise in this field and thought they could be of assistance. Len Harvey said he was interested and promised to contact Simon when they were back home.

Simon's idea was that if they could get a maintenance contract it could be very lucrative. Further, with some advertising and promotion he thought there were a lot of other companies that would welcome their expertise. If this could be achieved, he proposed they form a joint company and he already had a name in mind 'Your Problems Solved 24/7 Limited' to indicate they would offer a round the clock installation, maintenance and repair service. They left it at that, Harry would mull it over and come back.

Harry was intrigued, could it work, what were the risks, how much capital was needed, would they get the Maddox Hotel Group contract etc.? He and Amanda talked endlessly about the possibilities, good and bad, it would certainly be exciting and Harry had always had a hankering to be his own boss, so what should they decide? Amanda shared his enthusiasm so they came to the conclusion that, if Simon could definitely secure the Maddox contract, they would give it a go.

The next thing was to see if The Maddox Hotel Group were interested or not. So a meeting was arranged for Simon and Harry to meet with Len Harvey at their headquarters, a luxury office complex in Park Lane. Over coffees Len gave them a potted history of The Maddox Hotel Group explaining that some thirty years ago a group of five wealthy Americans decided that London was an ideal location for hotels, highlighting how many fabulous hotels were already established. Not scared of competition their aim was to set up a chain of luxury hotels to attract those who enjoyed the finer things in life. They were then introduced to Mike Blank their senior manager in charge of maintenance onto whom they would report. He went on how they had appointed Christies, the leading agent in the hotel business, to find them hotels that could be purchased. Condition of the hotels was not important because they intended to completely remodel them and to extend where planning permission allowed. The first acquisition was The Belvedere Hotel in Paddington, London W2, owned for over 30 years by a Mr and Mrs Bond. It was in a sad state of repair, the accounts showed it was making losses so it was relatively easy to agree a price. The place was totally gutted, planning permission granted to build a 30-room extension, the name was changed to The Haven Hotel and it opened eight months later as one of the finest, if not the finest, hotel in the neighbourhood. This set the pattern for future acquisitions. It was at this stage that they appointed Len as managing director.

Over the next few years other hotels followed: 'The Albany Hotel' renamed 'The Retreat Hotel' in South Kensington, London SW10, 'The Ashbury Hotel' renamed 'The Harbour Hotel' in Bloomsbury, London WC1, 'The Alder Hotel' renamed 'The Sanctuary Hotel' in Putney, London SW15, 'The Out Field Hotel' renamed 'The Hideaway Hotel' in Tower Hamlets, London, E3 and lastly 'The Grand Hotel' in Aylesbury, a little further out but a magnificent site and this they made their flag ship hotel with the appropriate name 'The Hotel'.

These had received similar treatment to The Haven Hotel, some with extensions and all decorated and furnished to the highest quality. They prided themselves in the culinary presentations; every hotel had at least two cordon bleu chefs.

Mike Blank then gave a report on the various problems they were currently experiencing regarding the maintenance of the electrical and mechanical services. They had attempted to employ technicians and do the work internally but this had been a disaster. So they had entered into an agreement with a maintenance company based in Wandsworth, South London. This had improved the situation but only slightly. He enquired of Simon and Harry as to their expertise and how they would tackle the problems if they were appointed. With a bit of political licence, they ran through their training and subsequent work experiences making them very impressive, stating that if they were appointed their first priority would be to investigate each of the six hotels and prepare a report as to their recommendations.

Len Taylor summed up saying that they would first be commissioned to prepare a report on the six hotels for a fee of £3,000 per hotel and if this was found to be satisfactory they would be offered a 5 years' contract starting after the three months' termination notice that had to be given to the existing contractors. He stressed that the contract would be between The Maddox Hotel Group and a limited company that would have to be incorporated with a share capital of at least £20,000 and adequate insurance cover. This was agreed upon and after yet another cup of coffee they left determined to get things under way.

They agreed that time was of the essence, i.e. strike while the iron is hot. Simon had no time problem but Harry took the remaining three weeks of his holiday entitlement to get things sorted. They agreed that Simon would report on security, heating, health and safety while Harry would cover air conditioning, electrics, fire alarms and lifts. They would allot three working days to each hotel starting with the hotels in acquisition order.

The first hotel was 'The Retreat Hotel' where they met Mr Williams, the manager, a down cast looking man in his early 60's, whose suit looked as though it had seen better days. He had been informed of their visit and welcomed them with open arms stating how pleased he was that something was being done, expressing how the present contractors had made things worse, rather than better. It was a very involved three days' session, with so much to cover but at the end they were pleased with themselves.

Without a break, they covered the rest of the hotels with similar experiences and their final report ran into 352 pages. It laid out their findings, recommendations that included the installation of CCTV cameras in all strategic locations and estimates of costs if things were to be put right. The report was delivered to Len Harvey and a further meeting was called, which only Simon could attend as Harry's work commitments precluded him, he thanked them for their prompt action which he found impressive as he did with the report. He produced a draft contract for discussion and with some amendments, suggested by Simon, Len instructed a secretary to amend it. This was then signed by both Len and Simon on behalf of he and Harry, the proviso being that Simon and Harry had to set up a limited company with a share capital of at least £20,000 and adequate public liability insurance. The start date being in three months' time.

They discussed the terms of the contract that Simon agreed to and would start in three months' time after notice had been given to terminate the existing contract.

Chapter 5

Setting Up the Business

Harry had to work out his three months' notice, so left it to Simon to deal with the formalities that he did at a meeting with Joe Payne, a chartered accountant recommended by their bankers. Joe seemed a typical accountant, dark suit, boring tie, smartly lacquered hair with his brief case and rolled umbrella in the corner age about 40-50. Simon was impressed how easily Joe understood what was required to set up a limited company. Harry and Simon were to be the sole directors, limited capital £20,000, Joe's firm to be the auditors, dealing with all tax matters etc.

Now down to practicalities. They rented a two roomed office in Hackney, North London and employed a typist come secretary, Hilda, no beauty but highly efficient with a great sense of humour, but pity about her fizzy hair. Simon, whose forte was fostering contacts, had managed to attract the business of a property management company who were responsible for the maintenance of ten large office blocks in London. Whilst he was the entrepreneur, Harry was the boffin with many impressive letters after his name identifying him as an expert in many fields including lifts, escalators, air conditioning, heating, etc.

The business grew rapidly and the contract income was impressive. After only three years they were bursting at the seams so they relocated to a suite of offices in the stylish Camden Lock area. The staff force now consisted of Hilda and her assistant Barbara, a pretty 20 year old, 4 technical engineers who operated under Harry whose main role now was supervisory, although he did continue to be the one responsible for after-hours call outs that arose infrequently. He didn't mind this as it kept his hand in. The offices were lavishly furnished, both had their own office, the two ladies occupied the spacious reception, the boardroom had thick pile carpet and an oak table that could sit twelve comfortably and an office for the technicians when they were in, which was only occasionally.

Amanda and Harry's combined earning supported their lavish lifestyle; they had sold their house in Fulham and, with the help of a large mortgage, had bought a beautiful penthouse suite just off Regents Park. Big gamble but the business was going so well there should be no worries!

Then one night his idyll was shattered.

Chapter 6
The Betrayal

Amanda was on one of her late night appointments. Normally Harry would have gone to bed about midnight in sure knowledge that she would join him in due course. Then the phone rang, it was their most important client, The Maddox Hotel Group. The air conditioning in their flagship hotel, simply called 'The Hotel', had packed up and because the autumn weather had been so hot, guests were complaining. So in good spirits Harry set off knowing it would be another satisfied customer. The hotel was only about 15 miles away towards Aylesbury so it was a traffic free journey listening to late night jazz.

He was met by Bert Hemmings, The Hotel's night manager, an elderly gentleman, smartly dressed in uniform, definitely ex-army, ruddy face who with a warm smile welcomed Harry. In reply to his informing head office of the problem, they replied informing him of Harry's visit. Bert informed Harry that the trouble appeared to be on the 12th floor but on alighting from the lift Harry could find no air conditioning equipment on this floor, so he took the stairs down to the 11th floor. He was just turning a corner when he was amazed to see Simon coming out of a room. Could Simon have also received a call-out message? He was on the verge of calling out when Amanda followed him and hand in hand they walked towards the lifts. Stunned he didn't know what to do. Surely there must be some explanation, but what? In his hesitancy they had disappeared into a lift.

What should he do? After pausing a while he chased after them but by the time he reached the ground floor they had disappeared. Stunned, he had a word with Bert who told him the Mr Thompson, as he knew him, occasionally booked this suite for him and guests, one of whom was sometimes this lady.

Bewildered, he finished repairing the air conditioning and made his way home, with a myriad of thoughts disturbing his peace of mind. When he got home Amanda was in bed asleep naked except for a sheet covering the lower part of her body. Not wanting to disturb her for fear of getting into some sort of awkward confrontation, he slipped into bed. Amanda stirred and lazily rolled over to caress him, which brought him to arousal, the result being they made passionate love before falling asleep.

Chapter 7
What to Do Now?

When he awoke in the morning, Amanda was already up getting their usual healthy breakfast, muesli, yogurt, smeared with honey and covered with milk, while listening to her favourite radio station, Magic. She greeted him with a big kiss and a hug and enquired if he had had a good night's sleep after his late night call-out. Everything seemed so normal it was surreal. *Did what he witnessed last night really happen or was it a bad dream?* He knew it wasn't. Still, thinking there must be a logical explanation he made a supreme effort to act normally, although a thousand questions were chasing through his mind.

Today they were due to play the semi-final of the Tennis Club Championship and were hot favourites to win. So her dominant conversation on the way to the club was all about the tactics they should play, which were she would dominate the net and he would cover the rest of the court except when she served then she would take the forehand letting Harry take the backhand, his strongest side. Try as he might, he couldn't concentrate so when the match started he couldn't remember whether he was expected to rush the net, whether to serve wide or down the middle and failed on many occasions to cover the centre of the court. Clearly Amanda was confused, Harry was the best player in the club and played for the county so what was going wrong? Their female opponent, Katie, was the one person in the club that always irritated Amanda with her supercilious attitude and jibes about their privileged lifestyle. Harry's serving was pathetic, he had four double faults and lost two of his service games, also his fabled backhand shots were awful, so many into the net and his lobs invariable went out of court so losing the first set 6-3 really irked. Trying to cover for Harry's obvious lack of form she ran like never before, covering the court, and through sheer determination and will power won the second set 7-5. Harry by this time found some form, his serving was powerful and the connection with Amanda was as it always was, with hand signals she knew where his serves would go, down the middle or wide. They had no trouble winning the final set 6-2. Katie ungraciously congratulated them on their win and air kisses were exchanged.

After a swim in the Club's pool and drinks with friends, they headed for home. On the drive Amanda enquired if Harry was okay considering his lack of form. Wanting time to collect his thoughts he put it down simply to the late night.

He made a decision. He had to find out more, so that evening he drove to 'The Hotel' for another chat with Bert. Without disclosing that the woman in question was his wife, he said that he wanted to find out more about 'Mr Thompson'.

Bert was intrigued and wanted to know why. Harry strung him a story about 'Mr Thompson' owing him money with the thought that if he could implicate him in an illegal business, he could put pressure to get the debt paid. Bert enquired how he could help then Harry discussed his plan as follows, "Bert

I'm a specialist in surveillance and would like to install equipment in the store cupboard next to the suite used by Mr Thompson, so I can see what he is up to. If you agree to this without any mention to your bosses, I will pay you £500 plus £100 for every time you phone me letting me know when he has booked the suite."

Bert, who had worked at the hotel for over 25 years and now nearing retirement thought this extra cash would supplement his pension and make his and his wife's retirement more comfortable. So, provided Harry promised not to let his governors' know, he agreed and the next day Harry installed the surveillance equipment with hidden cameras in the lounge and bedroom of the suite.

Chapter 8

The First Viewing

A fortnight went by before a phone call from Bert. During this time life continued as normal and Simon was as affable as ever, showing no signs of guilt or anything untoward. Bert informed him that Mr Thompson had booked the suite for this coming Friday night.

Coincidently, Amanda had said she had a midnight photo shoot for one of her major clients for an advertising campaign, which had to be shot in the dark. She left about 10 giving Harry a kiss goodbye saying she shouldn't be later than about 2am.

His pulse racing, he forced himself to watch TV for 30 minutes before setting off into the unknown future. Being in charge of maintenance, Harry had a key to the staff entrance and was in the store cupboard without even Bert knowing. Checking the camera's wide angles, he could see the whole of the lounge and bedroom. The first vision was of Amanda and Simon lounging on the sofa enjoying a glass of pink champagne. They seemed so relaxed and looked very smart in their respective designer clothes and in no hurry to do anything else, which Harry hoped this was all they were meeting for. But soon they stood up and embraced with passionate kisses and disappeared into the bedroom. When he switched to the bedroom there was no sign of them, just the sound of splashing, which he could only assume they were showering. They soon emerged towelling each other and when the towels were dropped they were both naked. It seemed all good fun as they laughed and fondled each other. But as he feared they entered into a sex session, the likes of which he had only witnessed on the occasional porn sites he watched on the Internet. First, Simon had laid towels on the dining table in the lounge and Amanda lay face down on them. Simon produced a bottle of scented oils and started massaging Amanda from her shoulders, and without haste worked down applying quantities of the oil to her waist then moved to massage her feet, gently working his hands higher spending a lot of attention on those erotic places.

All this time Amanda seemed to lay in a trance, then she started to writhe rolling over onto her back and implored Simon to enter her. What followed totally shocked him, his love making with Amanda had always been satisfying at least for him, but she had never been so active as she is now.

Harry's emotions swung from pure rage to disbelief, arousal and jealousy. Should he rush in and confront them? What good would that do? he pondered. Confused, he waited until they seemed contented and disappeared into the bathroom again. Not wanting to see any more he drove home, his mind in a whirl.

On the one hand he loved Amanda and life was good but could he ignore what he had just witnessed? He needed time to weigh up his options so he curled up in bed and when Amanda came home trying to cuddle to him he feigned sleep.

Throughout the next few days he tried to analyse his emotions, and be rational, be calm. His emotions were hard to analyse, he had to admit that stronger than rage and disillusionment was the excitement of the image of Simon using Amanda as his plaything. It was so erotic that he had an erection every time the image appeared. This heightened his sessions with Amanda who showed no resistance to anything he wanted her to do.

What were his alternatives? He had to consider his lifestyle, the business, and what would be the outcome if he tried to bring things to a halt? After much deliberation he decided that the best course of action was to do nothing for the moment. Nobody was getting hurt; he was sure Amanda was in love with him. These sessions were only spasmodic and he could revel in the eroticism of it all. However, he would suggest to Amanda that they go away for a well-deserved holiday to one of the smaller Caribbean islands. She gave him a big cuddle saying how thrilled she was with the idea and that she had already set her eyes on a new bikini. As a tester he suggested that they invite Simon to join them. He was surprised and pleased when she turned down this suggestion out of hand. He left it to Amanda to decide on the holiday destination and do the booking.

Amanda decided the world was their oyster; did they want a sporty action packed adventure or a chilled relaxing togetherness time? She liked the idea of a relaxed intimate holiday so she settled on the Maldives, Bandos Island Resort. From the details it looked perfect, white sand, aqua seas, plenty of scuba diving and water sports but giving the feeling you are the only two people in the world if the mood takes you.

Their flight was at night taking off at 22:45 so they had a lovely morning making love after Harry had brought back croissants from the local bakers to have with their coffee. Always wanting to be early, they set off in a taxi at 5 to get to Gatwick in time, to check in, allowing enough time to enjoy the Oyster Bar, then relax in the executive lounge, afforded to business class passengers, before departure. They both agreed that business class travel was like a holiday in itself. "More champagne vicar."

Amanda was so excited she couldn't stop laughing and kept saying how happy she was at the thought of being away with Harry, just the two of them. Harry on the other hand was truly looking forward to the holiday but was worried he could not keep what he knew to himself. He knew he had to try to forget it although this could be difficult.

The flight was uneventful, they both managed a little sleep waking at 4:30am for the landing at Ibrahim Nasir International Airport. After clearing customs, they were collected by the hotels limousine and whisked away to the hotel. The place was amazing, the sea so clear, tropical trees festooned the bright green lawns, everything so perfect. Their room was all you could hope for, spacious, French doors opening onto a private terrace, king-sized bed, mirrors on every wall, lounge and a shower that could accommodate four. It brought back memories of weekends when neither of them needed to rush out to work, they would shower together and bathe each other with such intimacy.

They were both looking forward to scuba diving and some pampering in the Spa. But for the first night they decided to have a wander around the resort and possibly eat at the restaurant or have room service. After a leisurely wander around, they decided to have a couple of drinks overlooking the sea. Perfect. They made use of room service and as neither were very hungry, just ordered smoked salmon and scrambled eggs.

The two weeks were flying by, they had swam, made love most mornings, enjoyed scuba diving in waters so clear and warm, viewing fish the likes of which they had never seen before, such bright colours and a variety of sizes. Every time they were back in their room they just could not keep their hands off each other, either showering together, washing each other from head to toe, which often lead to another urgent and amazingly satisfying love making session.

Amanda could not be happier, she couldn't help thinking how marvellous things were with Harry compared to the sessions she had with Simon where there was no emotion purely sex. However, this holiday had shown her exactly why they had been married for 12 years and why they were so happy. She had difficulty remembering how the affair with Simon had started, it must have been that Caribbean holiday. Now she realized the massive impact it would be if Harry ever found out it was going to stop.

Harry was having a great holiday, he loved Amanda more than she could ever imagine, which is why he was struggling so much with her infidelity. Seeing her with Simon and seeing how different the sex was, quite urgent, rough and even animalistic at times, did shock him but he had to admit seeing her like that did turn him on. Their sex life had improved, not that it was ever stale, but it had definitely perked up. He felt so confused but was coming to the conclusion that if he wanted his marriage to last the only way was to try and blot it out and hope that the affair would take its course and that it was a one off. He knew that if her affair with Simon continued their marriage could never be the same.

Drastic action was to follow.

Chapter 9

Another Viewing

He hoped this holiday had put an end to the Simon saga but a few weeks later, another phone call from Bert and low and behold Amanda had another late night business job. He was dismayed to think this was starting all over again. On the night in question, Harry was again positioned in his surveillance hide hole fearful of a repeat performance. But this time Simon was casually dressed in a cream shirt, pressed white trousers and white sneakers. In contrast Amanda was naked under a bathrobe. They were casually chatting and sipping pink champagne. There was a knock on the door and Simon indicated to Amanda to go into the bedroom, then he opened the door and welcomed in a black man, elegantly dressed, some 6ft. 2 tall, handsome, who Harry thought was in his late 30's. They shook hands and after a glass of champagne Simon ushered 'Max' into the bedroom where he apparently showered and emerged stark naked showing he was well endowed. He had ignored Amanda who lay sprawled naked on the bed but now she got up and embraced Max, kissing him French style standing aside to avoid his now erect penis. She got him to lie on the bed and began rubbing him all over with scented oils, applying an adequate amount to his erect member. Then she straddled him and positioned the tip of his penis into her vagina and started rocking back and forward.) Harry was mesmerized and watched her take the whole length. After what seemed like ages, Max lifted Amanda and positioned her over the dressing table and started paying attention to Amanda's rear. Harry couldn't take any more and went outside for fresh air and try to make sense of what he had witnessed. Again, his mind was in turmoil but he felt compelled to see what was happening. Max, obviously showered and dressed, was chatting with Simon while Amanda was presumably still showering. He thought he had seen everything but as Max was leaving he peeled off six £50 notes and handed them to Simon. Harry was astounded; did Amanda know she was being used as a high-class hooker? Was this how Simon was paying for his lavish lifestyle? including the new Porsche he recently bought?

Clearly, he could not let this situation continue. Rage now overtook all other emotions. Who should he confront first, Amanda or Simon and what would he say? Logic told him that he must find out if Amanda knew she was being used. If so, he would be disgusted and couldn't see how they could continue their marriage.

Further, this new situation made him consider Simon in a different light. It was one thing being cuckolded in sex but what about the business? What did he really know about Simon? They had met at university, got on well, enjoyed the good things in life and after going their separate ways had teamed up in business. By this time Harry had married but Simon appeared to be happy playing the field. Harry had never queried the business accounts that Simon regularly produced and as his substantial salary and bonuses were always paid on time, he never worried or enquired further. He decided he wanted to make discrete enquiries and his first port of call would be to the company's auditors who had looked after their affairs since inception.

The news he got from the meeting with Joe Payne, one of the partners, was quite shattering. Whilst Harry had always considered they had equal shares the fact was that they were held 60/40 in Simon's favour, and also his earnings were almost double of Harry's. The only word that came to mind was 'bastard'. Ever since they started, he had been led to believe they were equal but now any control he thought he might have over the business had vanished and he could be out voted on all matters including who were the directors.

What other dirty tricks had Simon been up to? He thought about the various clients and started to wonder why Simon was so protective of the Maddox Hotel Group. Harry had never seen the contract but just knew from Simon that it was profitable and demanded prompt attention whenever called upon. He decided to visit their head office in Park Lane and eventually got to meet Len Harvey. After a preamble about the amount of call outs, which Len Harvey went out of his way to say the service was much appreciated. Harry skirted around the contents of the contract and without any prompting, Mr Harvey was quick to justify why the charges were so low, because although not in the contract it had been verbally agreed that a luxury suite in The Hotel would be made available for them whenever required, provided it was free. So, this was how Simon could 'afford' a luxury suite!

To gather further information, he had another word with Bert to find out more about 'Mr Thompson's' use of the suite. He discovered that frequently there was more than one guest, sometime up to four including one or two women. Bert was tipped £100 in cash every time so he just turned a blind eye.

Obviously, Simon was a pimp and Harry was going to expose him but he intended to leave Amanda out of any ensuing scandal. Now that he knew others were involved, he would make maximum use of the surveillance cameras. Bert's back handers were raised to £100 for every phone call. The first call came four days later. He knew Amanda could not be involved as she was in Hawaii on a major promotions job and would not be back home for 2 or 3 weeks. He knew this could not be a ruse as he had phoned her many times to see how she was getting on.

On the appointed night Harry was in position early to see Simon arrive with a most attractive brunette. She was over 6 feet tall, elegant with a graceful body that curved in all the right places. After the customary glass of champagne and a shower, 'Anita' was shown into the bedroom. Not long after Simon admitted two swarthy Eastern looking types exuding wealth by the cut of their clothes and the amount of jewellery they wore. Harry judged them to be in their forties. When Simon suggested they shower they refused, but when reminded it was part of the deal they relented. It did not appear that Simon trusted them because he asked for the payment of £2,000 up front. They argued that they would not pay until satisfied they would get all that had been promised. After again some argy bargy, they relented and paid over a wad of fivers. What Harry witnessed and recorded does not warrant describing; suffice it to say that 'Anita' would not be walking home. After the Eastern gentlemen had gone, Simon paid her £500 and escorted her out, presumably to call her a cab.

Now that he had this evidence, should he go to the police? Not wishing to include the recordings of Amanda's involvement, he decided more evidence was needed and therefore he would wait for another occasion. This came along on the following Sunday, and again Harry was in position when Simon arrived with an Oriental woman of mature years, well the wrong side of forty who he called Kim. She refused champagne, showered and came out naked displaying a perfect body with well-defined muscles, a wonderful golden bush and small but firm breasts. They then sat discussing the 'visitor' who he called Mr J and instructed her in what was required. She nodded in full understanding and donned a bath robe. When Mr J arrived, Kim welcomed him with perfect charm. He must be in his 70s and rather frail. She led him into the bedroom and when she tried to unbutton his shirt it was clear he was very ill at ease. She was so gentle and encouraging that soon Mr J was naked and lying on the bed still showing signs of discomfort. Still with endearing talk she covered him with oils and massaged every part of his body, but it took her a long time to get him aroused and the culmination was not long in coming. Kim led him to the bathroom where apparently, they both showered. Mr J returned to the lounge fully dressed with a smug smile on his face, obviously well satisfied. On leaving he handed Simon a cheque the value of which Harry could not guess. However, he did record Simon giving Kim what looked like £600 in fivers.

Chapter 10

The Mission

Harry now considered he was on a mission, he had to bring Simon to justice, but how to do it was a conundrum. One thing he was certain of was that Amanda could not have any further association with Simon. So, he planned first of all to meet her boss, Ben Harvey, who had met a few times before at the Company's functions, to find out more of these late night shoots. Ben was the epitome of a successful ad man, smart casual did not do him justice, his spotless white silk shirt, gold cuff links, perfectly creased trousers, and with his engaging smile could have been a male model.

Ben, with a firm handshake, made Harry most welcome and over a cup of coffee, in company's board room, discussed the weather and how the test match vs Australia was going. Asked what was the purpose of his visit. Harry said everything seemed to be going okay but would like to know how Amanda was fairing and what the future held. He was pleased to hear Ben rated her highly and he hinted that it wouldn't be long before she was offered a directorship.

Nothing had been mentioned about the late night shoots and Harry didn't want to divulge too much or raise any suspicions so he casually asked whether any of the staff had to work nights. Ben thought for a moment then said he could remember that about 6 months ago it seemed to be appropriate to record a scene for a particular client in the early hours when the streets were clear, but that was a rare occasion. Harry thanked him and as he was about to leave Ben said Amanda should be returning from Hawaii in a week or twos time.

This revelation did nothing to lighten his misgivings, therefore he could see no alternative other than confront her with all he knew, but in such a way as not to ruin their marriage. It would be tricky, tact would be of prior importance but the problem would have to wait until she returned home.

The ideal scenario would be if Simon disappeared, no more disturbing thoughts of Amanda and he was confident he could carry on the business alone. One thing he had found out was the value of the cheque from Mr J. It was while they were in the office; Simon was in discussions with a potential new client in their boardroom, leaving his jacket on his office coat stand. Harry had extracted his wallet and found the cheque for an astonishing £10,000. Mr J's name was W K Althorp. The name rang no bells but Harry would not forget the name.

Wishful thinking but Simon was not about to disappear, at least not of his own accord. Harry thought about all the books he had read and films he had seen where unwanted people were made to disappear mostly because they were murdered or frightened enough to make them run. Murder ran through his mind, poison, accident, falling off the office roof, blunt instrument, but was quickly discarded as the thought of killing anyone with a gun, a knife or hit over the head with a blunt instrument brought the reaction, "Don't be absurd. I am no killer and certainly do not relish the idea of spending a long time as a guest of Her Majesty."

If he found out more about Simon's nefarious activities, there may be something there that he could use to threaten Simon, with a full report to the police if he did not disappear out of their lives. So, he hit upon a plan, although he was expert in static surveillance, he was no private eye adept at discovering anyone's secrets, he would employ one. Looking thorough Yellow Pages, he picked "Herbert C. Malone" being impressed with the slogan "Skilled in unearthing those hidden secrets". After a phone call, he visited Malone's office expecting it to be seedy like those in many detective novels, tucked away in some rundown part of town, dingy cluttered office with one ancient lady who looked after is affairs, constantly worrying about lack of funds. It was therefore with some surprise that he found Malone had a suite of offices in Highgate, elegantly furnished. A charming lady asked him to wait in the waiting room while Mr Malone finished a phone call. Soon he was showed into Malone's office and sitting behind a polished walnut desk was a gentleman in his 50s, smartly dressed in pin stripped suit, what looked like a military tie and bright red hankie in the top pocket. With a firm handshake Malone introduced himself as Herbie and asked Harry to take a seat. Coffees were brought by another lady, then Harry set about telling Herbie the whole story answering in depth all questions raised.

At the end Herbie leaned back in deep thought with his fingertips pressed against each other. He then gave his summing up. Firstly, he thought Harry's surveillance recordings could cause more trouble to him than Simon, as they were illegal and even if given to the police, they would unlikely bring a case on that evidence alone but file it away for possible later attention. The fact the Harry had only recently discovered the fact that he was a minority shareholder worried him as it showed how naïve he had been all those years ago and it would be difficult to bring a case about this aspect. However, the females in the videos intrigued him as it hinted of criminal activities that could be the basis of the police getting involved, stressing that everything relating to Amanda would be deleted.

Herbie suggested the best way to incriminate Simon was to find out what he was up to and if there were any criminal activities, prepare a report to take to the police.

Harry thought this was a good idea but was mindful of the costs. Herbie explained that his fees were £500 per hour for him and £300 per hour for the other staff plus expenses. He would not hazard a guess as to how many hours were involved as it was a case of how long is a piece of string. However, he promised that he would give regular written reports and the agreement could be terminated immediately at any time Harry decided. Herbie seemed so professional that Harry paid over the £5,000 retainer. Herbie then showed Harry around the offices introducing him to his two female PAs, Veronica in her 50s (possibly named after Veronica Lake, Alan Ladd's wife both on and off screen) and Margaret, blond, busty and beautiful. Both elegantly dressed and exuding charm and competence. In a separate office, he introduced George as his right-hand man whose expertise was gathering information on various people and tracing missing persons. George was in his late 20s, 6 feet tall, blond, and handsome with piercing blue eyes, Adonis sprang to mind. In George's office, Herbie said that to start the investigation they required a full list of all business clients, telephone records of the business and if possible those of Simon's mobile and details of any of

Simon's known associates or friends of whom, Harry realized, he knew little. The next day Harry delivered all the information needed.

Chapter 11
First Report

Harry was most impressed because the first report arrived two days later. George has tailed Simon who at 21:44 had entered The Wimbourne Club in Curzon Street.

Chatting to a doorman, dressed in his very smart liveried uniform who introduced himself a Stuart, he learned this was an exclusive male only club for the very rich. "Ladies" were only admitted as guest of members. When George asked if he knew the gentleman who had just entered, he found out it was Mr McFarlane one of the owners. Stuart was evasive on further questions just saying there were other 'women' in the club but would not elaborate.

George hung around 01:18 hours, when Simon left. During this time observing comings and goings, some, presumably, members arrived on their own, a few ladies were ushered into the club by Stuart the doorman. A few 'ladies' left during this time that George had tried talking to without success, as they all pushed him away and hurried off. He got the distinct impression that they were all afraid they were being watched. However, he surreptitiously followed the last to leave back to her home deciding it was not appropriate at this time to approach her, so just made a note of her address.

Chapter 12

Amanda's Shock

Amanda was now home from Hawaii, showering Harry with presents, a colourful Hawaiian shirt, silk ties and a beautiful Rolex watch plus much hugging and kissing. What a perfect wife, no way could he let things slip back, not even for an occasional night out. He waited a day to let her settle down to get over any jetlag. He had booked a table at their favourite Italian restaurant, Il Palagio, overlooking the Thames which he thought would be a reasonable setting to disclose all the facts he had. But on reflection, not knowing how she would react he decided that any in-depth discussion would be best done in the quiet of their apartment so the reservation was cancelled.

At home, he poured them both a glass of Champagne and sat her down next to him of the sofa. Amanda sensed something was up, she pondered whether he was in business difficulties, or anything medically worrying him! So, it was a massive shock when Harry opened with, "My darling I know all about your affair with Simon."

"What the fuck are you talking about?"

"I have seen you two in The Hotel and in fact have some videos."

Yelling she shouted, "How dare you spy on me, you're nothing but a peeping Tom." and got up ready to storm out.

Harry had prepared for such a reaction and knew he had to stay calm, although boiling inside, not be accusatory and be understanding although he didn't understand at all. He held her by the shoulders and in a calm voice, "Amanda please sit down and hear me out."

She sat there motionless just staring out the window. "Sorry love but there are things that I know you are not aware of."

Petulantly she said, "Like what?"

His next remark was like a bombshell, "Did you know that he was using you as a high class prostitute?"

"Don't be so bloody absurd." Now he discloses to her how closely he had been viewing their liaison by informing her that he had seen the third party although avoiding any reference to the man or what they had been up to.

She really went on the attack screaming, "You're lying just to make me feel more guilty. Simon is not like that." He could have shown her the whole videos but that would have been embarrassing so he asked if she would like to see a clip, which was only of the money changing hands. She hesitated for what seemed like an eternity then gave the slightest of nods. It took just seconds to view it on their computer and it was obvious she was dumbfounded, then she burst into tears sobbing her heart out. Harry put his arms around her when she started to mumble that it had started as a prank then she got carried away with the eroticism of it all.

Not knowing how to take it from here Harry said, "Let's go eat and I want you looking gorgeous." Still tearful Amanda disappeared into the bedroom. About 30 minutes later she emerged looking absolutely stunning. Her deep Hawaiian tan made her long legs, in 6" high heels, look amazing and the short skirt left little to the imagination. Her silk blouse was Bond Street oozing expense and although diaphanous, did not show her braless nipples. Also, she seemed quite composed and her old confidence restored after dinner of tiger prawns, steak Chateaux Briand and rum truffles washed down with a couple of bottles of Dom Perignon.

Harry wanted to know about her trip to Hawaii but thought she may think he was prying so avoided any mention. However, she told him what a wonderful place the island of Oahu was, where she stayed at The Surfrider Hotel with her balcony overlooking Waikiki Beach, being able to watch the masses of surf riders zooming in on the huge waves, many of them standing on their boards with what seemed like effortless ease. She recounted how she had had a go but failed miserably when not a single wave would pick her up.

On the drive home Amanda was pensive and it was impossible to know what she was thinking. So, Harry waited in silence long enough knowing she would open up at some stage. As soon as they were in the apartment she turned to him and in a most serious tone, the likes of which he had never heard before, said, "I know it takes two to tango and I am ashamed at the part I played but what Simon has done is despicable and must not go unpunished." This certainly was not the reaction he had expected but it now appeared she was firmly on his side. So, he now told her about the other incidences at The Hotel, his chats with Bert, his meeting with Herbie, the first report and the meeting with the company auditors highlighting the fact that Simon had engineered control which meant that if Simon learnt of any plot to disgrace or harm him he could vote Harry out of the business, which would be catastrophic to their finances and life style. Amanda sat in stunned silence for a few moments and then asked Harry what he proposed doing. He said there seemed to be only two alternatives, one, do nothing and carry on without any further involvement on her part or two, somehow make Simon disappear either by getting him sent to gaol or flee to avoid disclosure. He did not mention the third alternative, Murder.

Amanda rose, took him by the hand, lead him to the bedroom and said, "Let's have a good night sex and ponder the problem tomorrow." *What a splendid idea,* he thought and hours of passion followed.

Chapter 13
Second Report

In the mail, next morning was the second report from Herbie. George had visited the woman he had followed knocking on her door at 13:00 hours. Had to knock three times before a bleary eyed young woman, the one he had tried to talk to earlier, opened the door. She looked at him in total surprise and asked what the hell did he want at this ungodly hour? He charmingly assured her it was past midday and that all he wanted was a few minutes of her time. Although sceptical she was intrigued by his good looks, quite different from the men she had to associate with recently, and after being assured he was not a policeman, let him in and introduced herself as Zoe. The flat was small, just two rooms, one dovetailing as kitchen, dining room and shower room. It was basically furnished with no personal items, except a framed photo of what he assumed were aged parents and their two daughters plus an image of Jesus Christ affixed to a wall. Otherwise the flat was neat, tidy and functional.

To start with George kept the chat general, learnt that she came from Latvia, that the photo was of her parents and her sister, Natasha and that she had been in England 6 months. Asked why she had come, her shoulders drooped and she looked sad saying that originally, she had come on the invitation of her sister who had been in London just over a year. However, when she called at the address Natasha had given her, she was told by the then occupant, a Mrs Wilberforce, a lady in her sixties, that Natasha had moved out weeks before without leaving a forwarding address or phone number. Natasha had seemed to leave in a hurry because many of her personal belongings had been left behind. Mrs Wilberforce was a pleasant lady saying that she had kept these belongings in case Natasha returned but agreed that Zoe could take them.

Not knowing what to do and with little money she went to the local police station. Their attitude was that many foreign women travelled elsewhere when they couldn't find work but the desk sergeant said her call would be registered. Asked for her address he was surprised she had yet to find lodgings. In the few personal belongings of Natasha's was a card from The Wimbourne Club. With no alternative, she paid a visit and was warmly met by a well-dressed middle aged man in pin striped suit, regimental tie and well-polished black brogue shoes. He introduced himself as Bob Watson the day manager of the Club. She showed him a faded photo of Natasha and asked if he knew her. Yes, she had visited the Club a few times as the guest of a member who he would not name but had not been seen for a few weeks. They chatted for a while, and when he found out that she had nowhere to stay suggested she contact Mr Costas to see if he had any spare rooms at his guesthouse. Bob Watson also said that if she was looking for work there were always opportunities for beautiful ladies at the Club. She was wary, thanked him and left. Mr Costas did have a one bed room at a reasonable rent that she could afford for only four weeks. Having no papers, she found it impossible to get a job and didn't want to go to the Job Centre, as they would ask too many questions. So, when her small amount of money ran out she had gone back to the Club. Bob Watson again made her welcome and explained that the job would be entertaining members while they were at the Club by serving them drinks and refreshments when ordered.

Having no alternatives, she started 2 days later and was supplied with beautiful smart clothes, fashionable but not too revealing. In her spare time, she was allowed to watch TV or read in the staff rest room, nicely furnished with comfortable divans. It appeared that the Club was for relaxing, watching horse racing and other sports on the two large TV screens plus gambling, the popular games being Blackjack and poker. All the dealers were beautiful ladies dressed in the style of airhostesses.

After about a week, one of the frequent members named Simon had taken her in the lift to a bedroom on the 3rd floor. He told her to undress and when she refused he struck her hard across the face knocking her onto the bed. Again, he ordered her to undress. She was scared but again refused. He dragged her by the hair, punched her in the stomach and left her lying on the carpet. She lay there whimpering and on the third order, she stripped standing there using her arms to cover up as best she could. He then threw her a bottle of scented oil and told her to massage the oil all over her body which she did while he sat relaxing in an arm chair just watching. When he seemed content, he used her like some common whore making her perform sex acts that were totally alien to her and made her retch. When he had finished, he told her this would be her daily treatment until she knew how to treat members and their guests properly. She was left totally ashamed and confused. She showered, dressed and thought of how she could escape. She discovered the door was locked and the windows where all shuttered also they had taken her passport.

No matter how she pleaded, this treatment went on for days, sometimes three or four times a day and with different men, some young others old. Eventually this Simon told her she was ready to meet her 'patron'. She was instructed to put on the new clothes he had brought and to look her best. Later he came back, inspected her then took her to a well-furnished suite on the first floor where she was introduced to a Mr J, smartly dressed but fairly old. It was explained to her that she now 'belonged' to Mr J and that she must do all his bidding. If there were ever any complaints she would be severely punished and possibly handed over to the police as an illegal immigrant. Further she would be evicted from her flat that Mr J had kindly agreed she could keep while other women had to live with their patrons.

When he had left the room, Mr J told her in a very kindly way not to worry as his needs were few and his passion was just to have the company of a beautiful woman. He also said that if she were good he would move her out of the tiny flat she now had, into a luxury three-room apartment he owned not far from his luxury suite in Vanderbuilt Apartment in Maida Vale. All he wanted of her was to visit him whenever requested.

These visits always took the same course. Mr J would politely ask her to do menial household chores, like vacuuming, dusting etc. while completely naked. Never once did he try to touch her, but many times asked her to pose while he took photos and as the sessions progressed so did the exposure to the camera. While cleaning one day, the post arrived which she picked up. She was surprised that none of the letters were to a Mr J but all addressed to Mr W K Althorp.

Mr J liked to tell her of his life in the oil industry and made many enquiries of her life in Latvia. During these chats, she tried to find out about her sister but he could add little to what she already knew except he suspected that she now had a patron. Asking about 'Simon' she learnt that he seemed to be one of the owners, but who really owned the Club was a mystery. He liked the Club, it was an excellent place to relax and he enjoyed a game of poker. He did not know how girls were recruited but had heard some talk of a country estate that the girls visited.

The report ended saying that George's next assignment was to try to locate the country estate and find out more about the 'patrons'.

When they had both read the report, Amanda and Harry sat in silence for some time, obviously assimilating their thoughts. She was first to speak, "Simon is a bastard, we have to do something so I have to get closer to him while he expects nothing to try to find out more about his business." Harry thought this was too dangerous and was totally against such an approach. She assured him there would be no sex but silently made her mind up to go ahead with her plan.

Chapter 14

Amanda Confronts Simon

Simon had not been in touch with her since she had left for Hawaii, so knowing that Harry was away on business, she phoned for him at their office and when informed he was out, asked to be put through to Mr McFarlane. "Hi Simon, I heard Harry is out. Why haven't you been in touch?"

"Pressure of business and a lot of things going on however I would like to meet up again so shall I book our suite?" he replied.

"Nice idea but how about lunch and a chat? Can't wait to tell you about the fun I had in Hawaii." They agreed to lunch the following Thursday at The Belle Restaurant in Covent Garden.

Amanda had not told Harry what she was up to as she wasn't sure in her own mind where things were heading. During lunch the conversation was light hearted, just generalities telling him about her holiday and it wasn't until coffee that she went on the attack saying in a quiet voice but emanating much venom, "Simon why did you use me as a whore?"

Taken aback he replied, "What on earth are you talking about?" Lying she said that when coming out of the bedroom she had seen Max hand over quite a sum of money.

She went on, "As you know I was mystified when you didn't join in as you said a threesome would be fun."

Off handily he said, "Darling, one has to earn a living to survive."

Feeling her anger rising she retorted, "You bastard I'm in a mind to report you to the police for pimping as I bet I am not the only one you have used."

With a supercilious smile Simon said, "I don't think Harry would be too pleased with the photos."

Amanda said, "You lying sod, you didn't take any photos."

"Darling I always take photos for insurance in case anything like this happens."

And from his inside pocket extracted one photo saying, "This is just a sample. Would you like to see it?" With apprehension, she reached over and took it. Her face showed absolute horror as she saw herself lowering onto Max's erection. The camera must have been located in the headboard. In a rage, she tore the photo into pieces. Lounging back in his chair with a smug smile he said,

"Darling I have many copies and even more graphic ones so don't do anything silly as even if they don't upset Harry I am sure Ben Harvey would enjoy showing them to your clients."

Amanda with desperation in her voice said, "You wouldn't dare."

Simon retorted, "Don't push me too far as you cannot believe the lengths I can go to."

With tears in her eyes she fled the restaurant hearing his last jibe, "I'll be in touch."

Her mind was in turmoil. What had she stirred up? The only positive thought was that apparently Simon had no idea that Harry knew the truth. But what if he did show them to her boss? Should she tell Harry what had happened? No, she would try to sort out a plan of her own in due course.

A few days later Simon phoned, "Darling, would you like the photos?"

"Of course, you stupid bastard."

"Well here's the deal. I have a wealthy Texan who got a thrill poring over your photos and would pay handsomely for a night with you. So, what do you think?"

With scorn she retorted, "I trust you about as much as I would trust a rattle snake. After you had pocketed the Texan's money you would then cheat me."

Simon with a hurt tone said, "Darling you know I am a man of my word. Anyhow what choice do you have if you want to save your marriage and your job?"

Her rage showed in the tone of her voice when she shouted, "Bollocks" and slammed the phone down. When she had calmed down a plan started to formulate in her mind.

Chapter 15
Amanda Formulating a Plan

The next day she was off to an assignment in Switzerland, where she was met at Geneva Airport by Frederick Lingberg the producer of the advertising film they were going to make about ski equipment and clothing. He drove her to Hotel d'Angletere on the banks of Lake Leman. It was amazing, clearly, he was well known as, presumably, the manager, made a fuss of us clicking his fingers to a bell boy to take my bags, real five star. Her room was fabulous with a balcony giving views of Mont Blanc.

She looked forward to getting to know Frederick as he seemed very friendly and although he was quite a few years older than her he exuded charm and had a silky voice that she could listen to all night. She pondered on what she would wear for the occasion and decided on her figure hugging trouser suit from Gucci, complimented by a peplum fitted jacket to accentuate her waistline and her favourite shoes, the highest possible Christian Louboutin patented stilettos. Not to overdo the makeup, scarlet lipstick the same colour as the stilettos, a pair of diamond stud earrings and her TAG Heurer watches. She thought this might do the trick, who knows where the evening may lead?

Frederick was waiting for her in the restaurant and was taken aback by how elegant she looked and the way her slender legs looked in her cigarette trousers set off beautifully by those fashionable high heels.

That evening they dined in the Windows Restaurant, it was clear that Frederick was well known by the way the Hotel's maitre d made them welcome and escorted them to a table in an alcove overlooking the lake.

Over aperitifs, Frederick complemented her on how gorgeous she looked and hoped they would have a lovely evening. The menu was extensive with dishes she had never heard of, so she asked Frederick to choose for her. With great aplomb, he ordered Gravelux followed by Lobster, Thermador, always a favourite, he explained, finishing with a chocolate mousse complemented by Bollinger champagne.

She loved listening to his accented English while he explained in detail the film they were to make before moving on to ask about her life, was she married, any children, her hopes for the future etc. In return, she enquired about his life, yes, he was married, two daughters who had emigrated to Australia, apart from the business his only hobby was a gun club. This caught her attention wanting to know more about this hobby, which led on to enquiring how easy it would be to buy a gun in Switzerland. She was disappointed by his reply that it was almost impossible unless you had an official permit. Various scenarios flitted through her mind, would Simon back off if confronted with a gun?

The evening ended with a nightcap in the bar, a peck on the cheek and bed. Nothing more!

In the morning, Frederick collected her in his 911 Porsche and off they went to that beautiful ski resort, Courchevel where they met up with the film crew from Box One Limited. There were female and male models, wardrobes full of ski wear, masses of skis and other paraphernalia. Thankfully the weather was perfect so the shoot was finished in 3 hours.

On the drive back, she broached the gun subject again with Frederick, except this time enquiring if a gun could be bought illegally. He was intrigued as to why she was so keen to buy a gun but sympathetic when she told him a yarn about being stalked by some crazy who threatens to rape her. He told her there was a gun shop in town and that if she approached Mr Winnersh, the owner, and tell him that she has chatted to him and plus a bit of bribery he may offer to sell you a pistol.

The next day she located the gun shop and got chatting to Mr Winnersh who spoke perfect English. She told him about Frederick and spun a different yarn that she lived in Germany's Black Forest and was pestered by wild boars digging up the garden. She wanted a pistol powerful enough to kill them. He understood the problem and suggested a rifle would be more effective but she said a pistol would be preferable as the pigs came up close to the house. He was dubious but took a greater interest when she offered him £100 over his asking price. He took her into the rear of the shop where there was a shooting range, showed her various pistols, advising that for her purpose a .22 should be sufficient. She chose Smith & Wesson Model 422, had a few practice shots in the shooting range and agreed a price. He said the gun was not traceable back to him and that if challenged, would deny any involvement.

She pondered, *How could she get the gun back to England?* She put it in a parcel with two boxes of Havana cigars and posted it to her office address keeping her fingers crossed that it wouldn't be detected. It didn't and arrived no problem. The cigars were given to Ben and the gun spirited away. Would she be able to use it? She thought back to the time she got retribution against the two men who had terrorised her back in her concluding *yes, I can do this*.

Amanda's Return

Harry met her at Gatwick airport giving her hugs and many kisses saying how much he had missed her. He updated her about how well the business was going and the fact that Simon had kept his distance spending much time away from the office. On the tennis front he had lost in the singles final to a young upstart that he should have eaten for breakfast.

As soon as they were indoors they kissed, cuddled then like frantic animals almost tore the clothes off each other, a prelude to passionate lovemaking.

He had not updated her on the meetings he had during her trip.

Harry and Amanda were due to attend a presentation dinner at the Tennis Club for the retiring chairman. Getting ready he couldn't find his gold cuff links, presumably Amanda had put them somewhere safe, not waiting her to return from a last minute shopping trip, he had a go at trying to find them. He searched all the bedroom draws, bedside cabinets then the wardrobes where he found a hat box at the back. On opening it, he was amazed to find a revolver, where on earth did this come from? As soon as Amanda returned, holding up the revolver his first words were, "Darling what the hell is this?"

Calmly she explained, "Ever since the trouble with Simon I have been worried that he might take steps to harm us and it is just a protection." He thought it didn't ring true but accepted the explanation with good grace and off they went to the dinner.

Chapter 16

3rd Report

It was about a week later that the third report arrived from Herbie. George had bugged various Club members' cars, traced Simon and one other to a country estate in Essex, known as Rosebury Manor. The security around this estate was like Fort Knox and although he couldn't get in, with his powerful night binoculars he clearly saw one half of the building had all the windows barred through which he could see many women but couldn't make out whether they were distressed or not. In the other half, various men seemed to be lounging, drinking and some playing cards. The photos he took were long-range, and didn't reveal anything untoward.

George had traced two other members to presumably their houses. Both were large properties again with high class security systems. He had also called on W K Althorp, who was obviously worried when George hinted that he might be party to an organized gang sex trafficking in foreign women. W K A admitted he had paid £10,000 for the privilege of membership to The Wimboure Club and accepted that he had used Zoe, but hastily added that he had not laid a finger on her. On the promise that George would leave his name out of any investigation report, he revealed that after being thoroughly interviewed by two gentlemen he was accepted as a member and that for a further £5,000 he could become the owner of a beautiful woman who would effectively be his slave to do with as he pleased. He did not like the idea as his only sexual encounters had been in a hotel suite with a very attractive Oriental lady who he knew as Kim. She was the one offered to him, so it seemed natural to let her become his friend. George was pleased that he had sufficient evidence and promised Althorp he would do his best to keep his name out of his report. In return, he did not want any of this to be discussed with any one at the Club.

The report ended with a suggestion that Harry should visit him to discuss the next stage.

This meeting took place the next day. Herbie suggested that the next move should involve some breaking and entering, which although not in his province, he knew a man who could. Harry said, "Tell me more."

So Herbie continued, "His name is Bill Smith, well not his real name, but he is an expert at entering high security buildings and obtaining sensitive information. I have told him about the Club, the Essex estate, the houses of the two members and Simon's apartment. He does not come cheap, but is prepared to undertake the job for £2,000."

Harry scratched his head and considered whether it would be worth it, and then asked, "What would I do with the information?" Herbie said that provided there was sufficient incriminating information, it could either lead to blackmailing Simon, but to what end? Or presenting a case to the Serious Crime Squad. He was friendly with the head of the SCS, Jim Carter, and knew he would be interested if, as Herbie suspected, there was trafficking in women. Harry asked whether they had enough information to go to the SCS now. Harry said possibly, but he thought the information was a bit flimsy and may end up being filed away for future use. Harry thought *what the hell, for another £2,000, let's go the whole hog.*

As Amanda had not mentioned the matter for some time, Harry assumed she had come to terms with the situation and therefore he thought it best not to tell her of the new developments.

Chapter 17
Simon's Proposal to Amanda

A large envelope arrived for Amanda at her office marked, "For addressee only." Opening it with trepidation, there was a smaller envelope marked *'for Ben Harvey, if you dare'*. Of course, she opened it in the privacy of the ladies' loo and was horrified to pull six explicit photos including the one of her mounting Max. She thought *'what is this madman up to?'*

She didn't have long to find out. The phone rang, "Darling what do you think of my little present?"

She had anticipated that something like this would happen and made sure all private calls were recorded, she didn't rise to the bait and remained silent. Simon continued, "I know you can hear me and must know that I am serious about my Texan friend. So if you don't want a whole bunch of photos in a beautiful album delivered to Harry and your boss, you had better think seriously of my offer and as an added incentive there is £1,000 in it for you,"

She replied, "You are despicable, you leave me no choice other than to go along with your plan but I want £2,000, all the photos with a written statement confessing that you took the photos and that you have deleted them from your computer, plus, that if they were ever to come to light you

76

would pay me the sum of £50,000, before I take a stitch of clothing off. Even then I don't trust you not to come back for more and if you do, I'll kill you."

Simon, "Darling don't be so suspicious and it could be fun."

She enquired when this assignation was to take place to which he replied, "It will have to be Thursday week as our Texan friend is out of the country. So be at our suite at eleven o'clock and look your best."

Amanda said, "I'll be there."

He rang off with, "Deal done. See you there." Amanda smiled to herself, as the first part of her plan had been set.

Chapter 18

The Breaking and Entering

Monday morning another report arrived from Herbie, enclosing the report from Bill Smith that read:

Report by Bill Smith – Sunday 16th

FRIDAY 14th 6:00 hours. Entered the Wimbourne Club. There were three men on the premises on the ground floor eating breakfast while watching BBC news. Made thorough inspection of the office on the third floor. In both the safe and filing cabinets there were incriminating documents copies of which are attached. (These documents included agreements with clients, that included the names of the women sold to them and the fee paid). There were no women on the premises but there were five small rooms suitable for holding someone captive. These rooms were tastefully furnished, they could have been designed by The Ritz's interior designers.

SATURDAY 15th 04:20 hours. Entered Rosebury Manor, the estate in Essex. The property was in two parts, separated by a central Oak panelled entrance door. On the left were three men fast asleep. The windows on the right were barred and the internal doors securely locked, took me sometime to gain entry. There were five women all asleep in different rooms. Their personal belongings did not contain any passports, but from such items as postcards and photos it appeared that four are eastern European and the other from Thailand. Two of them had severe bruising to their faces and arms. There was no office as such but there was a register of the kind used in hotels recording guests, in and out. Attached is a copy of the most recent page which shows that five have not been marked 'out'. All earlier pages are marked 'guests out' except in two incidences there was just a line through the 'out' column.

SATURDAY 15th13:00 hours. Entered Willesden Court in Hatfield, the home of a Club member named Suliman Hazkic, he was not at home. It is a large house heavily secured and an initial search found nothing untoward. But on further investigation, I located a securely hidden locked door leading to a basement. I did get entry but there was a further locked and bolted door that I could not open. I knocked gently and a female responded but not in English. With my limited knowledge of languages, I discovered she was Polish and locked in with two other women. As best as I could, I told her that I was with the police and help would arrive within a day or two, in the meantime act as usual, do not let them know you have been visited.

SUNDAY 16th 11:30 hours. Entered Simon's apartment, he having left at 11:00 for his health club. In his safe there were many photos of women of all varieties, which could only be described as pornographic. There was also a list marked 'Private clients; see copy attached.

I have purposely omitted any reference to how entries were gained to these premises but it is unlikely that anyone will be aware they have been 'visited'.

Yours, signed Bill Smith

The attachments were:

From The Wimbourne Club (a) Full list of members with names, address and notes of their standing. (b) List of women giving names, nationality, their sexual ability and who bought them. (c) List of employees including four directors one of which was Simon McFarlane.

From Rosebury Manor. The last page of the register.

From Simon's apartment. List of private clients.

Harry phoned Herbie saying he had studied the report and wanted to know the next step. Herbie was very impressed with the report and said the case should now be presented as soon as possible to Jim Carter, as the women could be in great danger. Harry agreed and a meeting was set up for early next morning. Following this a full report was delivered to Jim Carter.

Chapter 19

All Hell Breaks Loose

Jim Carter informed Harry and Herbie that the Wimborne Club had been under suspicion for some time. Going on saying that firstly they could find nothing illegal about the company set as they had everything in order. Accounts registered on time, all employees taxed under PAYE. The only dodgy things was that B shares that had no voting rights, were issued to members for their subscriptions instead of being treated as income thus avoiding VAT and corporation tax. The Inland Revenue had been informed so it was in their court.

What had raised their interest were reports from various sources of the number of young women seen on the premises. They had enough information to build a case but he thanked Harry and Herbie for this latest information, which strengthened the case and would allow them to arrest all those in any way connected. He asked whether Bill Smith would give evidence, Herbie said he thought it was doubtful; Jim nodded with a knowing smile. He said no problem because all the documentation mentioned would be discovered in the raids to be planned. When they left they werc assured they would be kept informed.

Later Harry got a message from Jim Carter informing him that the raids had been planned for the early hours of Friday morning. His excitement mounted but stuck to his decision not to tell Amanda although he sensed that she was uptight about something because while appearing her normal self on the outside, she was often wrapped up in deep thought as though something was bothering her.

Amanda had told Harry that on Thursday evening she was playing an evening indoor tennis tournament, but should be home about 23:00. On that night at 22:30 she sent him a text message saying *Sorry, urgent call from Ben. Client wants night photo shoot. Be home about 2am.* He was alarmed, could the affairs be starting all over again or was this to do with her plan? Then a thought struck him, *what about the gun?* It wasn't in the hatbox. His first thought was phone Jim Carter who considered it so important he brought the planned raids a couple of hours forward.

******

At 22:00 hrs, Amanda entered the suite to find Simon there with the Texan, introduced as Buddy, waiting for her. True Buddy was impressive, could have been John Wayne's younger double. But this was not what she was there for. Simon said, "Amanda you look gorgeous, I'm sure you will not disappoint Buddy."

She retorted, "To hell with all that clap trap, where are the photos and my money?" Buddy looked quite amused as Simon handed over two envelopes. Amanda opened both, counted the money, looked at the photos then turned to put them in her handbag. Simon & Buddy looked in horror as she turned levelling the pistol at them. Simon was the first to speak, "What the hell do you think you are playing at?"

Amanda, "If you think a little shit like you is going to ruin my life, you have another think coming." Buddy started to say it was nothing to do with him and started for the door.

But Amanda levelled the gun at him and said in a soft but chilling voice, "Stay where you are unless you want the first bullet."

He froze. Simon, shaken but confident nothing would happen said, "You wouldn't dare shoot, it would be heard and you would go down for murder."

Amanda, "I'll take my chances. All the suites on this floor are empty and there are no security guards."

Simon not liking the situation thought that fast action was his best bet so when the gun was pointed at Buddy he made a charge for her but she was quicker and let off a shot that ripped through his right thigh. He went down like a stuck pig screaming, "You fucking cow. What the hell do you think you are doing, call an ambulance."

In a calm voice she replied, "You deserve everything you are going to get." and turning to Buddy, "Buddy, pick him up and place him on that chair." Shaken he did as he was told while Simon continued screaming with his thigh pouring blood all over the carpet. With this done, in an icy voice, she said, "Now strangle him."

"Christ, I'm no killer."

Amanda retorted, "Either you do it or you will be the first the die."

"You're mad," he yelled. The next shot went so close to Buddy's head it nicked his ear and blood began trickling on to the collar of his white shirt. Confused he put his hands around Simon's neck applying only minimal pressure. Amanda now with venom in her voice and the gun pointing at his chest, "Harder unless you want to go first."

He was at loss as what to do. Simon was now begging and pleading, "Amanda I'm sorry just stop this madness and I'll make everything okay."

Just then the door to the suite was flung open and in rushed Jim Carter followed by three policemen and Harry. Dumbfounded Amanda flopped into a chair and meekly handed the gun to Jim Carter's extended hand. Buddy who had gone as white as a sheet was so relieved when led away by a policeman. As for Simon he kept whimpering, "Thank you, thank you." Before being read his rights when charged with trafficking in women, obtaining immoral earnings and warned that even more serious charges may follow. Of course, he pleaded his innocence while he was stretchered to an ambulance attended by two policemen.

Jim Carter said, "You two had better get off home but come to the station tomorrow to make a full statement. As you know Harry, me and my team have a very active night ahead of us."

The police raids basically confirmed the information that Herbie and Harry had provided with a major addition. In the garden of the Essex property they discovered the bodies of two young women buried in shallow graves, this tied in with the register found on the premises.

******

Amanda in an emotional state started asking masses of questions, but Harry told her to let the dust settle until they got home then all would be revealed. The drive home was in silence, but after pouring a glass of wine each he told her all about the last reports from Herbie and explained that he had not told her before because he thought she had buried the experiences and didn't want to be reminded. He then went on to explain that he had found out from Ben Harvey that there was no late night appointment, then discovered the gun was missing. Putting two and two together he knew something was up. He had phoned Jim Carter to explain the situation and the advice was that they get to the hotel ASAP. A skeleton key was obtained from reception and the rest she knew.

Harry said, "Amanda, now it's your turn to fill me in with what you were up to." She looked sullen and in quite a defensive voice told him that if she had known what was going on she would have waited, but told him about the threatening phone call from Simon, leaving her confused as to see any way out of the mess so long as Simon was alive. She loathed the way Simon has used her, so she planned to go along with his suggestion with a twist that she would get the Texan to strangle him and frame him for the murder or shoot them both and make it look like a quarrel that went wrong. She would disappear and hope no one traced it back to her. She realized it was far from a perfect plan but couldn't see an alternative. *What an incredible woman to think up such an outlandish scheme.* thought Harry.

Chapter 20

The Interviews

What a traumatic evening. They drove home in silence, deep in their own thoughts thankful for the kind words of Jim Carter but mindful of tomorrows interview. Once home, they started comparing their thoughts and there was not much light at the end of the tunnel as they agreed they were both guilty of serious crimes. Further, it was highly likely that the media would relish reporting on such an intriguing story and Amanda was scared of the effect the whole story would have on her career. What would her work colleagues and more to the point her clients think of her? Would they change their minds about offering her a directorship? Would she be fired? Would she go to gaol? Whatever way she looked at it, it was a nightmare.

Harry worried about his business. The parting of Simon would be no more than a ripple but how would his clients react especially the Maddox Hotel Group. If he lost their business it was doubtful that the business could survive in its present state.

Harry assured Amanda that every tape on which she appeared had been destroyed (this was not quite true, he had placed them in a bank's safe deposit box in case he wanted to see them again sometime in the future) but the rest would be handed over to the police. When he asked her, what had happened to the photos that Simon had handed to her, she assured him they are safely hidden away where no one would find them. "Why were they not destroyed?" he enquired,

"They may be needed if it became necessary to take legal action against Simon." She replied. He said this was absurd as it could act against her but she insisted they stay hidden.

It was 3am before they got to bed, mindful they had to be at the police station in seven hours' time. A kiss and cuddle, no inclination for sex, followed by two very disturbed nights' sleep.

Over toast, marmalade and coffee they tried to envisage how the interview would go. So many variations were possible and although Jim Carter seemed friendly and understanding, last night he has a duty to perform to prepare a full report, so they decided to get their stories matching but what to include and what, hopefully, could be buried. If it starts to get incriminating clam up and wait until we have discussed the whole matter with a lawyer. Smartly dress they set off at 9:30.

The desk sergeant knew they were coming and ushered them straight in to an interview room where Jim Carter joined them. He started by thanking them for the information they had provided, which was the final chapter in the police's investigation that had been going on for the last two years. The investigation was part of a national one that had been launched following a report by The National Crime Agency (NCA) highlighting the growing problem of people trafficking, the main areas being child abuse, slavery both commercially and privately and the sexual exploitation of women. This latter area was the subject of this investigation.

The police had isolated various organisations in the UK who had contacts abroad, the major players being in eastern Europe, with Romania high on the list and Nigeria, where it was known that gangs enticed women to travel to the UK, charging up to £50,000 with promises of good job prospects. They charged a minimal down payment the balance being a loan to be paid off over a few years and for this they were supplied with passports and travel documents. This invariably led them being forced into prostitution to pay off the loan and there was always the threat of being reported to the authorities leading to being deported.

Jim Carter said he would have to officially interview them separately and asked Amanda to wait in the reception. The interview went like this:

JC: "Harry you know both of you are guilty of some serious crimes and although I will do my best to keep it to a minimum, there are questions that need to be answered and this interview is being recorded."

H: "Thanks for explaining what the police have s been doing and I'll do my best to co-operate."

JC: "I know you told me enough so we could arrest Simon and many others but for the records, in your own words tell me what was your involvement."

H: "The major client of our business is The Maddox Hotel Group and under our contract we have to give them 24 hours' service when necessary. Well back in August, as the out of hours' contact, I received a phone call stating that the air condition in The Hotel, their flagship hotel, had gone down and guests were complaining. So naturally, even though it was gone midnight, I attended. It was while there I glanced Simon leaving the hotel and had disappeared before I could call him. This was very strange and got me wondering if he had received a similar call-out, but when I asked him in the morning, he made some cock and bull story about just checking up on a few points. This didn't ring true, so I decided to meet with Len Harvey, the MD of The Maddox Group with whom Simon had concluded our contract. I just asked him if everything was going okay, he said everything was fine but without any prompting he seemed to think I was enquiring about our charges, because he said the reason for the reduced fee was because although not in the contract we had been promised a suite in The Hotel for any of our staff providing availability. Well, I was shocked so made further enquires and from Bert the hotel's night porter I learnt that Mr Thompson, as he knew him, often used the suite for meeting with various ladies.

"I then met with the Company's auditors who had set up our company and learned that the shares were not held 50/50, but 60/40 in Simon's favour. So before confronting him I decided to get some evidence of his dubious activities and arranged for Bert to let me know when he was to use the suite. Unbeknown to anyone, I installed the surveillance cameras and the rest you know."

JC: "I understand that but where does Amanda fit in?"

H: *(This story he had rehearsed with Amanda)* "Well, before we got married, they had had an affair and he had some very explicit photos of her that she thought he destroyed, but some months ago he started to threaten to send copies of these photos to both me and her boss, unless she would have an affair with him. She was appalled and flatly refused but the threats got more serious and she got herself into a right old state. She didn't tell me what was going on but decided on this fanciful notion that if she scarred him enough he would back off, hence the gun idea."

JC: "But how did she know he would be in that particular suite at that particular time?"

H: "I had told her about my enquires so she knew he sometimes used this suite, so she contacted him about his threats and said she would co-operate on promise of him retuning all the photos and he suggested they meet at this suite."

JC: "Because it seems reasonably plausible it is unlikely we will be bringing any action against you but those third parties appearing on the tapes you have given us may sue you for libel or some such crime."

H: "You've no doubt seen them and can you believe anybody wants to be in any court case either as defendant or accuser?"

JC: "Okay, please go into the reception and ask Amanda to come in."

Amanda comes in and sits in the chair JC beckoned.

JC: "I've heard Harry's story now tell me in your own words what happened."

Her story reiterated Harry's almost word for word.

JC: "Where did you get the revolver from?"

She told him about her trip to Holland and how the gun was posted to England.

JC: "Incredible. Harry told me about your reasons but how come you shot him in the leg and this other guy whose ear you nicked?"

A: "I only had the gun to threaten him but when I got there he had this other man with him and it seemed this guy thought I was to be his plaything. I said he must be mad and demanded the photos, but when he got angry and started to come towards me, I fired a shot which nicked this other guys ear, but he kept coming, so I had no alternative other than to shoot him but not fatally. Luckily you turned up at this time otherwise I do not know what would have happened."

JC: "Well I'll prepare a statement for both of you and we'll see what happens."

With this he said goodbye to both of them and wished them the best of luck.

Chapter 21
The Tennis Final

They felt quite relieved that the interviews had gone well, which made them feel relaxed and looking forward to the finals at the Tennis Club. They were up against Valerie and Rob Henshaw newly married 18 year olds who had gained quite a reputation as aggressive players. So far in this tournament they had not dropped a set, so a hard match was envisaged.

Their planning had been positive, each realising the part they had to play, two key elements would be Harry's serving and Amanda's dominance at the net plus their all-round stroke play.

It soon became obvious that the opposition were fast and covered the court at lightning speed on top of which they had good technique. Games went with serve to 5 all, Harry held his serve so Valerie to serve to save the set. She had hardly made a mistake but at deuce she double faulted, then Harry made a fantastic cross-court volley to win the first set.

The second set was just as hard fought and at 6 all, went to a tie break. Incredibly both men had dropped a serve so it was 5 all when Amanda reached for a high lob, missed it and fell heavily backward so 5/6 leaving Rob to serve for the set which he did.

It seemed that age would be a dominant factor in the deciding set but it turned out that Amanda and Harry's experience in tight corners proved to be the deciding factor as their composure kept everything tight. While their opponents let the tension get to them and the match was settled 6-2.

Having got the interviews behind them and winning the final they felt euphoric.

Little did they know what was to follow!

Chapter 22

Interview with Simon

Limping, Simon was brought from the cell to the interview room where he was soon met by Jim Carter and an assistant.

JC: "Well Mr McFarlane would you like to tell us about your involvement in this sordid business?"

Simon liked the idea of being the centre of attention so flippantly said,

S: "Do you want the long or short version?"

JC: "A full account would be helpful."

S: "Okay here we go. From being a nobody my life really took off when there was knock on the door. There was a young serious looking policeman who announced he had some bad news. I ushered into the lounge and asked what the problem was.

"It was clear that the lad had little experience in whatever he had to say and bluntly spurted out, 'Your mother and father have died in a plane crash.' In absolute shock, I tried to make sense of it. I asked what had happened but the poor lad had no further information so I thanked him and bid him goodbye.

"I had not been close to my parents since I moved to Norway but it was hard to think of life without them. I contemplated what had to be done which was soon answered by a phone call from Mr Richard, the family solicitor, who had been apprised of the situation and suggested we should meet as soon as possible to discuss what had to be done. Within the hour we meet at his office. Again, I had imagined a solicitor's office would be like those seen in many films, an old oak desk covered with files, papers everywhere and old fashioned furniture so was surprised to see a minimalistic office, a modern desk with nothing more on it than a computer, phone and a note pad. Mr Richard told me the story he had been told, my parents were on a holiday in Kenya, had taken a site seeing flight trip over Kilimanjaro when a sudden thunder storm had blown the plane off course forcing it to crashed into the side of the mountain, killing the pilot and the four passengers on board. It was not known whether it was a pilot error or a mechanical fault. The Air Accident Investigation Branch had already sent a team to investigate. The British Consular had already taken steps to repatriating the bodies.

"Do you want me to go on?"

JC: "Please do, it is getting interesting."

S: "Mr Richards got down to practicalities, first he explained that the Will was straightforward, apart from a few special bequests. I was the sole beneficiary and executor so it was my responsibility to arrange probate and explained that until probate was granted little could be done. This was all a foreign language to me so I asked if he could deal with this. He warmly accepted and informed me of his fee structure. I took a hard breath.

"Next, he talked about arranging the funeral which he thought would be arranged by the army pointing out that my dad was a general in his old regiment, The Green Jackets, and thought they would get in touch suspecting I would want a Military Funeral with all the pomp and glory. I had no idea my Dad had achieved such dizzy heights.

"A few days later a senior officer of The Green Jackets visited to discuss arrangements and costs of the funeral." It would be a full Military Funeral at The Magdalen Hill Cemetery in Winchester close to their barracks. They would take care of all arrangements and asked me if I knew of others who would like to attend. The officer told a little of my dad's history in the army and the many medals he was awarded, I'd never thought of him as a hero. I thanked him for taking so much off my shoulders and felt like saluting as he left, but didn't.

"Now it got boring as Mr Richards went on about me having to obtaining many copies of the death certificate, as they would be needed to present to banks, insurance companies and the like.

"Now to practicalities. We should visit my parent's home to take count of important documents, make a list of the contents and make certain it is secure. In due course a chartered surveyor should be instructed to make a formal priced inventory that would be needed for probate.

"On leaving the office I thanked Mr Richard for all his help and agreed he should take care of everything.

"The visit to my parent's house, bearing in mind I had not set foot in it for many years, was amazing. I didn't recognise any of the furniture everything was bright and new but down to business.

"Luckily my Dad had been meticulous in documenting everything of value, presumably in case of an insurance claim.

There were lists of their properties, stocks and shares, life policies, both his and Mum's jewellery, and anything of value, object dart ornaments, and more. The property portfolio consisted mainly of residential houses, two small office building but I found the most intriguing was reference to a freehold in Essex that was listed as a vacant previous residential school for girls. What on earth did they have this for?"

"While Mr R was down stairs I went upstairs wandering around the different room just admiring the contents. In their bedroom, I found a box at the back of a wardrobe stuffed with £50 notes. I suppose I shouldn't admit this but the temptation was great and thinking the government would get 40%, I hid it away for a further visit of which there were many.

"Everything went according to plan, Probate was received, all assets were transferred into my name, the funeral was a spectacular affair, all pomp and glory, regimental band, guard of honour.

"My only contribution apart from paying my share was designing the head stone that read *Thanks Dad for everything, always thinking of you' and mum's*. Shall I continue?"

JC: "Let's have a break for coffee." After, Simon continued,

S: "I sold the stocks and shares, cashed in all the life insurance policies, sold all the other assets including the properties except the Rosebury Manor the Essex ex school, the total result was a staggering £20,565,000 and this was after paying the inheritance tax. Whoopee I was now really on my way."

JC: "All very interesting but none of this seems to have any bearing on the case in question."

S: "You're quite right but it does lead on to what happened. It all revolved around the Essex school."

I wanted to find out why the Essex girls school had not been sold, so I arranged to meet the agent on site. The young lady estate agent, Jenny Seagrove showed me all around the place pointing out that it had not been maintained for a year, which she explained appeared to deter prospective buyers. Coincidently three gentlemen were due to visit at noon this day, so I delayed my departure.

These gentlemen arrived promptly at noon and Jenny gave them a tour. It was impossible to gauge their reaction, clearly they were interested and when they were introduced to me as the owner they wanted to discuss possibilities. The tall one whispered 'could you ask Jenny to leave'.

It all seemed a bit strange none of us rushing to say anything, a real pregnant pause; they were the first to break the ice by asking me why I wanted to sell. Not wanting to make out I was anxious to sell I told them I had plans to maybe reopen it as a private residential school. This created some reaction as they glanced at each other as though they were surprised. In return, I asked what was their interest. Who I gathered was their front man, said 'we run a gentleman's club that employs many ladies who we have to find accommodation for which is always a problem. At present, we have 5 houses but ideally, we would like to acquire a suitable building to furnish for the accommodation of about 15 ladies.

I found this dodgy but always interested in anything to do with the opposite sex, so I asked them to explain who they were. The tall good looking man, in a mid-European accent, introduced himself as Constantin Grozav from Rumanian

98

came over as a very friendly person anxious to please whom I thought I could do business with.

Valantine Ezenwa, a Nigerian, was built like a brick shit house, could have been a double for Idi Amin, I was surprised how gentle his handshake was for such a big person and spoke perfect English in a soft voice.

Then there was Hossan Mahoud an Egyptian, quite small about 5'6", who seemed to be humourless, supporting a floppy moustache and a permanent scowl. I took an instant dislike.

I reckoned all of them were in their late 40s.

Maybe this was the big mistake I made by suggesting that I visit their club for a further discussion. They seemed keen, so I duly arrived at The Wimbourne Club and was impressed by being met by Rosanne, a tall elegant brunette, as I stepped out of the taxi. The place took my breath away possibly like you when you raided.

The three gentlemen welcomed me, then Constatin took me on a tour of the premises, no need to explain as you know all about the place. However, I was intrigued about how many small bedrooms there were all in their own way, luxuriously decorated.

Anyway bit-by-bit they explained the real details of their business. The three of them had contacts in many countries that recruited young ladies with promises of respectable jobs in England for a small fee. When those that fell for this scam arrived they were kitted out with a fine wardrobe, shown a private bedroom. It was later they found out the real purpose, giving sexual favours to members.

I know I should have run for the hills instead I was excited. Knowing I was interested Valentine put forward a deal, if I put in the Essex property they would renovate it to accommodate up to 15 women for which I could have a 25% interest in the whole business. Of course, I mulled this over and thought what the hell let's have a go. Without enquiring I assumed they owned the freehold of the Club so a 25% interest seemed fair. After more discussions, the deal was done and it was actions go.

The rest you know'

JC: "Incredible, what a stupid man you have been, with such wealth why on earth did you risk everything? Anyways, thanks for being so honest but I have to caution you of the charges you will face. Will you be appointing a solicitor?"

S: "I hadn't thought of it but will give it some consideration."

The interview ended and Simon was taken back to the cell.

During the raids, the police had tried to round up all the employees at The Club, the country estate and the directors in their homes. They had arrested Simon and Patrick O'Connell but the other two directors had fled the country, Rakawi Kengani back to Nigeria and Jamal Owanel somewhere in the Middle East. All the personnel at both the Club and the Estate were taken into custody. Other arrests followed when the police rounded up twelve 'patrons' and took into care their 'slaves'

The stories the freed women gave were heart rending. Most came from the Middle East others from West Africa, a couple from Poland.

Chapter 23

Other's Arrests

At the raid of the Club, four men and three females were taken into custody. At the Essex estate 4 men and 13 women were also taken into custody. After brief interviews the three of the women at the Club and all 13 at the Estate were seen to be blameless and released into community care. The stories these women gave were heart rending. Most came from the Middle East others from West Africa, a couple from Poland. In due course, they all made statements that may be used in the various court cases. The general consensus was they had all been raped every time a member requested their company usually without rough stuff which only occurred occasionally, otherwise they had been looked after reasonably well.

Raids on the other directors' houses proved fruitless, the theory being that somehow, they had been tipped off about the raids and disappeared, possibly now back to their countries of origin, a case for Interpol, maybe!

Other arrests followed, the police rounding up twelve 'patrons' taking them into custody; their 'slaves' were released into community care before being questioned.

All those remaining in custody were charged with a combination of:

Immigration crimes
Physical and abusive attacks including rape.
Slavery, confiscation of passports.
Murder relating to the two female bodies found buried in the Essex estate.

The exception was W K Althorp aka Mr J who had only ever shown kindness to Zoe who subsequently became his wife.

The Criminal Prosecution Service were going to have a field day, so many individual cases.

The two women arrested at the Club stood trial but were found innocent.

Apart from Simon and two of the men at the Essex estate, everyone else including the 'patrons' were found guilty on all charges other than murder and sentence to between 5 and 10 years. All requests for bail were denied.

The 'patrons' included a high court judge, an MP and the head master of a local school.

On the charge of murder Simon and two on the men from the Essex estate were found guilty the sentence for all three being a jail term of not less than 30 years.

A leading firm of lawyers acted for all the abused women obtaining large sums ranging from £50,000 to £80,000 for all of them. Unfortunately, the trials went on for over a year so those who return home had to fly back for the trial date.

Chapter 24

The Media

Amanda and Harry thought the interviews had gone okay, hoping this was the end of the matter. No hope, worldwide media latched on to the story, it featured on many television programmes so everyone connected to the case were hounded for their side of the story. Luckily Amanda and Harry came out as the good guys, the couple that had been instrumental in bringing down a sex trafficking gang which lead to a major investigation into the slave trafficking trade. Much of this was thanks to Jim Carter.

They received many offers to tell their story refusing them all except for one television appearance on the ITV programme 'Good Morning' coming over as the crusading duo.

The Aftermath

Harry formed a new company "Troubles Solved 24/7." All business assets and the database were transferred from the old company. Possibly illegally but if Simon wanted to bring an action it would be dealt with when the time came, if ever.

Amanda was promoted to a director with a substantial increase in her salary.

Amanda and Harry put all their trouble behind them, renewed their wedding vows and even considered trying for a family. On the tennis front he won the men's singles title 3 years running and together they won the mixed championship twice.

Simon forever more walked with a limp. He wrote a long letter to them both professing his sorrow for all the trouble caused. Amanda did reply thanking him for keeping his side of the bargain relating to the photos (but had he hidden any away for future use!).

Herbie retired and George became sole owner of the detective agency making much use of the services of Bill Smith. Their lives became very exciting possibly worth a novel of their own!

Zoe's sister Natasha was found as one of the 'slaves'. It took months for her to recover from her ordeal but as soon as the trials were over they went home to Latvia.

The Windborne Club and Rosebury Manor had been boarded up. Their future is still in doubt, as ownership could not be proved.

When Jim Carter retired, he wrote a bestselling book about the sex trafficking gangs including a chapter on how Amanda and Harry played a big part in bring a major gang to justice. His final chapter was daunting when he expressed his view that all the time men desired prostitute these gangs, mostly from eastern Europe, would flourish.